MAYA

A Dress for Me!

by **Sue Fliess**
illustrated by **Mike Laughead**

Marshall Cavendish Children

Marshall Cavendish Corporation
99 White Plains Road, Tarrytown, NY 10591
www.marshallcavendish.us/kids

Pinwheel Books

Library of Congress Cataloging-in-Publication Data
Fliess, Sue.
A dress for me! / by Sue Fliess ; illustrated by Mike Laughead.
— 1st Marshall Cavendish Pinwheel Books ed.
p. cm.
Summary: Before school starts in the fall, a young hippo
tries to find just the right dress to wear.
ISBN 978-0-7614-6148-7 (hardcover)
— ISBN 978-0-7614-6149-4 (ebook)
[1. Stories in rhyme. 2. Clothing and dress—Fiction.
3. Hippopotamus—Fiction.] I. Laughead, Mike, ill. II. Title.
PZ8.3.F642Dr 2012   [E]—dc23   2011016404

The illustrations were rendered in graphite
and digital media.

Book design by Vera Soki
Editor: Marilyn Brigham

Printed in Malaysia (T)
First Marshall Cavendish Pinwheel Books edition, 2012
10 9 8 7 6 5 4 3 2 1

Marshall Cavendish
Children

For my Aunt Barbara and niece, Erin—
I love you from head to toe
—S. F.

Thank you, Candace, for teaching me
that dresses are interesting and beautiful
—M. L.

School is starting.
I've grown tall.
Time to buy new
clothes for fall!

"Should we shop now?"
I say, "Yes!"

Mom says I can
choose a dress!

Lots of choices
I can see.

Will I find a dress for me?

Rows of dresses,
wall to wall.
Watch me as I
try them all. . . .

Jewels that shimmer,

big pink bow,

beads and fringe
from head to toe.

Stripes and checkers,

spots and plaids,

ruffled trim with
shoulder pads.

Pointy collar,
    puffy shirt,

polka-dotted
poodle skirt.

Sleeves that roll up,
sleeves that tie,

sleeves like wings
so I can fly!

Shiny sequins,
lacy sash,

feather boa . . .
ballroom bash!

Satin, strapless,
for the prom.

"Too grown-up for you," says Mom.

Dress too baggy,

dress too snug.

This dress looks like
Grandma's rug!

Is it hopeless?
Should we go?
Mom says yes,
but *I* say no.

That one hanging—
way up high!
One last dress
I have to try!

Fancy fabric,
sparkly snaps,
swirly rainbow
shoulder straps.

This one's perfect!
Can it be?
Yes! This dress was
made for me!